BOONMEE AND THE
LUCKY WHITE ELEPHANT

Boonmee and the
Lucky White Elephant

BY JANE HAMILTON-MERRITT

ILLUSTRATED BY PHONGSUN

Charles Scribner's Sons,   New York

TO THE THAI CHILDREN
whom I've lived with and loved
during my years in Thailand

BOONMEE AND THE
LUCKY WHITE ELEPHANT

SOUTHEAST ASIA

1

Lotus Boat Wish

BOONMEE awoke with a feeling of anticipation. Now there were only two days and one more night to wait.

The warm tropical sun crept through the open door, shining on his face. As he blinked the sleep from his eyes, he looked over at his father, mother, and four sisters, still asleep on the floor under mosquito nettings.

He was excited because these were special days. There was so much to do and so much to think about.

Yesterday had been his tenth birthday and in two more days there was the Loy Kathong Festival. He slipped quietly from underneath the gauze netting and went outside where his gray-haired grandmother was squatting before a charcoal fire cooking the morning rice. This morning he had a special reason for talking to his grandmother alone. He had a wish that he wanted to make at the festival, but he was afraid. He knew that grandmother would understand his problem and would be able to help him.

Boonmee squatted beside his grandmother and scratched his brown big toe in the dirt. He must ask her. She would know what he should do. Finally he burst forth: "Grandmother, is it true that a wish comes true if the lotus boat gets safely to the Mother-of-the-Waters?"

The wrinkled, almost toothless old woman spit some red betel nut juice from her mouth and watched it melt into the sand. Then she looked down at her small brown-eyed grandchild. "Yes, my son," she replied, "it's true."

While he waited for his grandmother to get into a storytelling mood, Boonmee drew sketches of lotus blossoms in the sand with a stick. Some were small and dainty, and others were awkward and clumsy.

Boonmee loved to hear stories about the Loy Kathong Festivals when Thai people float miniature boats called *kathongs* to the Mother-of-the-Waters. During the festival the people make special wishes to send along with the *kathongs,* which are made of lotus petals and banana leaves.

Slowly stirring the rice, his grandmother began the story of a Loy Kathong wish that did, indeed, come true. "Many years ago, before you were born, before there were any children in this house, your mother wished for a child. But only spirit babies came."

"Spirit babies?" echoed Boonmee.

"Yes," she answered. "Babies who live less than seven days are only spirit babies. They belong to spirit mothers who leave them with a mother for a few days and then come and take them away."

Boonmee scratched out his lotus blossoms. He didn't like to hear about spirits because they always scared him.

"Your mother knew that if she didn't have a child soon your father would take another wife," continued his grandmother. "So, we made a Loy Kathong wish for a baby.

"Boonmee, it was eleven years ago at the Loy Kathong Festival that your mother and I secretly floated a special pink lotus boat on the *klong*. We stood there silently praying for our wish to come true as the lotus boat dipped and sputtered in the water. We held our breath, then it grew stronger and floated away into the darkness. It was a good sign, my son."

She leaned over to whisper to Boonmee. "Your mother never knew that deep inside the petals, I tucked my last gold coin for extra luck.

"Yes, it's true my son. A Loy Kathong wish can come true. You were such a wish. You were born before the next festival."

"Maybe she's right," thought Boonmee. "Maybe if the lotus boat does reach the Mother-of-the-Waters, good luck will come to the villagers. Maybe wishes can come true. . . . Maybe."

Boonmee began to draw lotus blossoms again with his big toe. He looked at his grandmother and knew that she would say no more. Whenever she had finished talking, it was her habit to begin preparing betel nuts for chewing.

He often watched her split small green betel nuts, take out the red centers, and crush them into a paste. She wrapped this red paste into a betel leaf and added a pinch of tobacco and lime. When she   *3*

chewed this, it made her teeth black. Boonmee wondered how red juice could make teeth black.

Both of them continued to squat in the early morning silence. The old woman, with her hair cut short like a man, prepared betel nuts. The young nut-brown boy idly drew sand lotuses and hoped that his wish would come true. He had been thinking of his wish for over a year. Last year at the Loy Kathong Festival he couldn't find the courage to wish it. Maybe he would have the courage this year.

Even though Boonmee was sure that his grandmother would say nothing else, he wanted to tell her one more thing. "Grandmother, Phra Kruu, the monk at the temple, tells me stories about 5 the big city at the end of the waterways many miles away. He says people from all over the world live there together. There's a green Buddha carved from jade and stairs that move. He tells me so many things that I can't understand. They're hard to think about, but I can't forget them."

He continued talking even though his grandmother didn't seem to be listening. "Grandmother, I want very much to visit that city. I wanted to make that wish last year, but I was afraid that it wouldn't come true.

"Grandmother!" he insisted, trying to get her attention. "Why did Phra Kruu say such funny things yesterday when he gave me the Buddha medal for my birthday? Why, Grandmother?" But still she paid no attention.

Boonmee held the small, reddish Buddha image in his hands ever so gently. He could still hear Phra Kruu telling him, "This will protect you and bring you happiness." Then Phra Kruu was whispering, and he seemed to say, ". . . Boonmee, you will have more luck than you can know, more luck. . . ."

Then Boonmee heard his waking sisters talking inside the house. He quickly rubbed out the lotus blossoms from the sand and put his newly acquired Buddha image in his pocket. He didn't want his sisters to know that he was thinking about the festival. He didn't want anyone to know about his wish, except his grandmother. He didn't even want to talk with anyone just now. It was nice to think about the wonder and mystery of grandmother's story. Before anyone else came outside he wanted to go to the family spirit house to make an offering.

6   The spirit house stood in a corner of the clearing that sur-

rounded his home on stilts. The spirit house was a small replica of a Thai temple placed on top of a pole. Its dark red paint was faded from the constant beating of the monsoon rains.

This morning the spirit house seemed forlorn. Boonmee was as puzzled as ever over its mysteries. There were both good and bad spirits, but often when he neared the spirit house, Boonmee shuddered as he remembered the stories of the angry spirits who roamed the countryside tormenting and frightening people.

Today he would try to forget the evil doings of the bad spirits and concentrate on making an offering to the good spirits. He began to gather wild flowers for the offering, picking white and purple orchids, and red and pink bougainvillea. Then from the safety of his pocket, he took out the stick of incense that he had been saving for this special day. He arranged and then rearranged the flowers and the incense to make them into the shape of a lotus blossom. With the grace he had learned from watching his mother and grandmother give offerings, he stretched up and fearfully placed the flowers and the burning incense near the opening of the small spirit house.

His mother's calling voice interrupted his mumbled pleas to the spirits. He backed away quickly, then suddenly stopped to whisper, "Good spirits, help make my wish come true." He turned and ran toward his mother.

Boonmee loved his mother, for she was kind and gentle and always spoke softly. But she didn't understand him the way his grandmother did. She was always too busy to talk with him. "Boon," she said hurriedly, "you can take the coconuts to market by yourself today."

Boonmee was glad that the path to the market was deserted. 　7

It was good to be alone this morning to be able to think. Dense foliage formed an umbrella over the small brown boy as he trudged along slowly under the weight of nine coconuts. The path was cool and smelled good, with the scent of the wild jasmine flowers and monkeys.

When he got to the market he would ask grandmother's friend to sell the coconuts so he could slip away quickly. He would go home early to see if the four giant pink lotus that he needed to make his lotus boat were still floating lazily in the *klong*. If he could only keep the water buffalo away from them for one more day, they would be his.

2
Finding the
White Elephant

WITH THE marketing finished, Boonmee hurried home. As he neared his house, he could hear the voices of many men. They sounded very excited. All the neighbors seemed to be there.

He approached quietly and listened to their conversation. "If we could capture him," he heard one man say, "it would bring good luck to our village."

Another man interrupted him. "Well, we don't know for sure there really is one out there. It could be just a rumor."

Boonmee slipped quietly under the house so he could listen without being seen by his father. "It's been years since anyone has captured one . . . just years," his father said.

Boonmee moved closer to the house steps where his father was sitting. When he got too close, his father spotted him. "Boonmee, it's time for you to take the water buffalo out to graze, isn't it?"

"Yes, Father," Boonmee answered politely. Then he blurted out, "Father, what's everyone talking about?"

"One of the farmers said that he saw a white elephant in the highlands. We aren't certain it's true, but if there is a white elephant out there, we want to capture it. Capturing a white elephant is a great honor."

Boonmee's eyes grew wide with excitement. "A white elephant! Will it bring good fortune like it did in the old days?"

"Yes, Boonmee. A white elephant would bring good luck to our whole country. Now run along and get that buffalo out to the fields so he can eat."

Before Boonmee could take the buffalo out, he had to make a little box for his Buddha image because he didn't want to lose it. He tore a piece out of a floppy banana leaf and quickly wove a small box. Then, with his Buddha safe in his pocket, he untied the big charcoal gray water buffalo and led him out from under the stilted house.

Almost every day Boonmee took Buffalo out to nibble the plants and grass that grew between the fields. He would climb on the animal's broad back and just ride along. Since there were no fences, it was his job to see that Buffalo didn't eat his way into any rice paddies or vegetable gardens.

This big, dark beast, who pulled the heavy plow before the rice planting and who later helped stomp out the rice grains at harvest time, was his father's prize possession. He was also one of Boonmee's best friends.

Since today was a special day, Boonmee wanted to decorate Buffalo, so he decided to gather some bougainvillea. The pink ones *11* were the prettiest. As Buffalo moved by the bougainvillea bushes, Boonmee pulled off bunches of the pink flowers and put them in the pocket made by his crossed legs. He would make a garland of flowers for Buffalo and string them between his horns.

As he started weaving the flowers, he thought again of the white elephant. Imagine, a white elephant near his village! Could it be real? Boonmee had often begged Phra Kruu to tell of the great Thai Kings of the past who fought with armies of huge elephants. He knew the stories so well that he could tell them to his younger sisters.

There were stories of elephants with magnificent saddles who carried great warriors into battle. Beside the giant feet of the elephants, Thai soldiers marched bravely, carrying their long spears. Atop the swinging and swaying elephants, riding right behind the huge ears, sat the elephant drivers. In the saddles, under the protection of tiered umbrellas, rode the army commanders. Several times in Thai history, Thai kings, leading armies of royal elephants, had marched against invading enemies.

Elephants have always meant a great deal to the Thai people and Boonmee knew that they were still national symbols of his country. White elephants would bring good fortune. Whenever they were found, they were given to the King, who kept and protected them so that his country and his people would have good luck.

The great courage of the elephant campaigns stirred Boonmee's imagination. Often, when riding on Buffalo's back, he would take a piece of bamboo and pretend that he was an elephant commander. Great enemies would advance toward him, and he would urge Buffalo to attack. With his bamboo spear, he would drive the invaders away and protect his village from the enemy.

12

With all the excitement—his birthday, the Loy Kathong Festival, and the rumor of the white elephant—Boonmee was in a mood for bravery and battle. With his heels, he urged Buffalo to move along. "Come on, Buffalo, let's head for those trees near the ravine. The enemy must be there!" he shouted.

Nibbling as he went, Buffalo worked his way toward the ravine lying in the rugged terrain in the distant hills. A small boy and a giant gray water buffalo whose horns were decorated with garlands of pink flowers skirted around the rice paddies, heading for

the highlands. The boy didn't look like a warrior, but he felt like one. He was going to capture the enemy! Buffalo didn't look like an elephant, either, but to Boonmee he was the biggest elephant of all.

Suddenly Boonmee's pursuit was halted by a mournful cry. Buffalo stopped short. His head went up, and his nostrils dilated. He lowered his head and gave a loud moan. The high-pitched call came again. Buffalo lunged sideways in fright and threw Boonmee to the ground.

Boonmee lay there motionless. He was scared. He watched Buffalo lumber away, his heavy head swinging from side to side. Buffalo was running away. Boonmee knew his father would be very angry.

With his heart beating fast, he lay very still. To make himself braver, he talked to himself. "Whatever it is in those trees is angry or hurt," he whispered. Afraid to move, he lay still as a snake in the sun. The cry came again, followed by heavy thrashing. Boonmee knew what must be in there—elephants! Only elephants made such heavy noises when they walked.

Boonmee didn't dare get up because the elephants might smell him, and if they were angry they might chase him. Silently he rolled over and took out the banana-leaf box from his pocket. The Buddha image was still there. He would be safe. Phra Kruu had said so.

Then suddenly the foliage parted and three huge elephants showed themselves. They moved in Boonmee's direction, but then suddenly turned and headed for the higher ground up north. Boonmee kissed the Buddha image. He waited until the thudding and thrashing sounds grew distant, then he started to get up to run home. The mournful cry began again.

"It sounds like an elephant," thought Boonmee, "but the elephants have gone."

He knew these woods well because he sometimes came here with his father. He knew there was a deep, narrow ravine just beyond the tree line. The noise seemed to come from that area.

Boonmee crawled forward. He had to see what was in there. With the Buddha image clutched tightly in his hand, he moved slowly toward the tree line. He picked out a tall, leafy tree with big branches. If he could just make it to the tree, he could climb up quickly.

"If I can get up that tree," he thought out loud, "I can see into the ravine." Boonmee inched toward the tree. The cry split the air again. "It's the cry of an elephant! It has to be!" thought Boonmee.

A few yards from the tree, he carefully put the Buddha image back into the banana-leaf box and tucked it into his pocket. Then he stood up and waited.

Nothing happened. He took a deep breath and ran frantically to the big tree. He shinnied up the trunk. He passed one big limb, then a second, and he stopped on the third one, about halfway up the tree. Boonmee tried to breathe quietly.

He stationed himself in a safe, comfortable position and started to look around. It was dark in the thick foliage. It was hard to see, so he listened. He could hear the heavy breathing of an animal. Then his eye caught a flash of grayish-whiteness in the ravine.

Something was caught in the ravine. He quickly climbed higher in the tree. From his new perch he could see right down into the ravine. The sad cry came again.

There were more moments of silence punctuated by the sighs

of heavy breathing. Then the grayish-whiteness moved into sight. It was an elephant! A very small elephant! It was trying to climb the side of the ravine.

Was this the elephant that his father's friends were talking about? But this one was just a baby. The little elephant tried frantically to heave his round body out of one of nature's most hazardous elephant traps—a narrow, steep ravine.

Boonmee was worrying about the baby elephant until a distant trumpet interrupted his thoughts. The big elephants were returning. Boonmee knew a mother elephant would never leave her stranded baby for long. He had to leave quickly. He had to get back to his house and tell his father. Father would know what to do.

He scrambled down the tree. With his head down, he ran like the wind toward home and help.

3
Eve of the Festival

"FATHER! FATHER!" he called, as he came in sight of his house. His father came running out to greet him.

"Father! Buffalo ran away! And I've found the white elephant!" Boonmee screamed to his father.

"You what?" answered his father.

"I've found the white elephant! The white elephant!" exclaimed Boonmee between gasps of heavy breathing. "He's caught in the deep ravine just inside the tree line where we look for betel nuts."

"Now, son, calm down. Tell me what happened," his father demanded.

"Buffalo was grazing near the tree line when suddenly elephants started trumpeting. It scared Buffalo and he threw me off his back. He was so scared that he ran away!" announced Boonmee. "I managed to climb up one of the big trees so I could see into the ravine. And inside the ravine is a small elephant. He's trapped. He can't get out. But, Father, he's a very small elephant. He's just a baby," announced Boonmee, almost in tears.

"Don't cry, Boonmee. We'll find Buffalo first, then we'll worry about this white elephant," said his father.

A few minutes later his father and his oldest sister headed out across the rice paddies to look for Buffalo. Boonmee went inside the house, where his grandmother and mother were sitting on the cool teak floor, talking and sewing. They had overheard Boonmee's conversation with his father, but neither of them said anything. Grandmother just looked at Boonmee knowingly and smiled.

That evening, as Boonmee was taking his evening bath in the *klong* with three of his sisters, a neighbor approached leading Buffalo. Buffalo looked very tired. Boonmee, with a sigh of relief, just lay on his back and floated in the cooling water.

All evening Boonmee watched across the rice paddies for his father and sister. At last he saw them moving slowly toward the house. "Father!" he shouted. "Buffalo is here! A neighbor brought him home!"

Boonmee ran out to meet them. His father put an arm around his young son and together they walked back to their home on stilts. They talked about the little elephant trapped in the ravine.

When it was very dark outside and time to go to bed, Boonmee crawled under his mosquito netting. After a few minutes, he poked his head out again. "Father, when you go to the ravine, may I go with you?"

Boonmee's father smiled, thinking how grown up a ten-year-

old boy could be sometimes. "We'll see about that later," he said. Right now, you'd better go to sleep. Tomorrow night is the Loy Kathong Festival and you'll be up late. Go to sleep."

Long after his father, mother, and grandmother were asleep and the kerosene lamp was extinguished, Boonmee still stared out the open door into the dark night. He couldn't sleep. Quietly he crawled out of his cocoon of netting and went outside to sit on the steps.

Skiffs of clouds darted across the moon and stars. Gusts of wind came and went like the darting clouds. Buffalo rubbed his sides against the poles of the house, making a creaking noise. The geese and chickens beneath the house occasionally fluttered their wings as they moved about in search of different resting places. When the wind died down, Boonmee could hear fish and frogs splashing in the *klong*.

It was exciting to sit all alone in the darkness. He listened for the forlorn cry of the baby white elephant who was trapped in the ravine. He couldn't hear anything, but then maybe the ravine was too far away for him to hear. What would the little elephant eat? Boonmee thought that he might change his wish tomorrow night. Maybe he would wish that the baby elephant would be safe.

Then he thought of the lotus blossoms beside the fourth coconut palm. He had forgotten to check them tonight. The first thing in the morning he would look to see if they were safe.

Suddenly the moon, clear and silver, escaped from a cloud. He took his Buddha image out from the folds of his sleeping sarong. "Please, Lord Buddha, make my lotus boat reach the Mother-of-the-Waters. Please."

Boonmee sat silently until the moon was tucked in for the night under its cloud blanket. Then he quietly stole back under his mosquito netting.

23

4

Making the Lotus Boat

"BOONMEE! Get up!" chirped his littlest sister. She poked at him to get his attention. Boonmee sat up quickly. It was late—he had overslept. He put on his khaki shorts and ran out to the *klong*. As he raced along the *klong*, he searched for his lotus blossoms.

He couldn't see them. They were gone! Some water buffalo had probably eaten them. What would he do now? Those were the biggest and prettiest blossoms on the *klong*. He had watched them for days and knew they would make a lotus boat that would sail forever. Now they were gone.

He turned slowly from the water and walked back to his house. As usual his old grandmother was squatting outside the house, preparing her betel nuts for chewing. As she greeted him a good morning, he saw a heap of pink and green beside her.

"Grandmother," he cried, "where did you get those pink lotus blossoms?" She continued to cut the green betel nuts, exposing their red insides. "Grandmother," he repeated. "Where?"

Grandmother stretched out her skinny arm to Boonmee. "Come here," she said quietly. "Early this morning, before anyone was awake, I went down to the *klong* and picked these lotus blossoms for you. Everyday I watched you go down there by the fourth coconut palm and sit for a long time. I went to look, too. You're right, Boonmee. These are the loveliest lotus blossoms in all Thailand."

Boonmee squatted down beside his grandmother. She pushed aside the betel nuts so he knew she was in a mood to talk. "I thought that I might help you weave your lotus boat for tonight," Grandmother told him. "Let's make it so beautiful that Lord Buddha will help it down the many miles of waterways," she suggested as she began separating the green lotus leaves.

Skillfully, she tore the leaves into strips and began weaving an elaborate green boat. It was high on both ends and had a wide base. It was wide enough to carry the lovely pink blossoms. Boonmee noticed that his grandmother held the leaves very close to her eyes. It seemed funny, but he didn't say anything because he knew her eyes were very bad.

Suddenly Grandmother stopped weaving. "Boonmee, do you know that your father went to the village this morning to see if he could organize some men to capture the white elephant you saw yesterday?"

Boonmee just shook his head in silence. He didn't want to interrupt her.

"If the white elephant is caught," she continued, "and if he is healthy, our village will give him to the King. That's the tradition. 25

That means that our King and his Queen will probably come here to accept the white elephant."

Boonmee stared at his old grandmother's faded brown eyes. She was excited, and he hadn't seen her excited in a long time. "But, Grandmother, the King and Queen will never come to our small village. There isn't even a big road, and they live so far away in the city at the end of the waterway."

"Perhaps not, but they will surely come to the capital of our province. The Governor will give the white elephant to the King and the Kingdom." Grandmother paused for a moment. then asked softly, "Have you ever seen pictures of the King and Queen?"

"Yes," answered Boonmee. "There's a picture of them at school. Our Queen is young and beautiful."

"Son, my friends in the village say that now the people of Thailand do not have to lie flat on the ground in front of the King. They say that the King is young and has changed all that. I've never been outside of our village, Boonmee. If your father and his friends catch the white elephant, maybe we can go to the provincial capital and I can see the King before I die."

Grandmother was speaking in a hushed whisper. She wasn't really talking to Boonmee—she was just thinking out loud. After a few moments, she began to prepare her betel nuts. That was the signal that she had no more to say.

Boonmee had never seen his grandmother so excited. He hoped his father would be lucky and capture the white elephant. Then his grandmother could see the King before she died.

Silently, carefully, Boonmee and Grandmother made the lotus boat for the festival. They had almost finished when they heard the excited chatter of men's voices come from the trail. Boonmee's father

appeared in the clearing with about two dozen men, armed with coils of ropes, stakes, shovels, torches, and bundles of banana leaves. They all stopped in front of the house while Boonmee's father went inside to get a coil of rope and a shovel. Then they moved off across the rice paddies heading for the hills.

Boonmee stood and watched them disappear hurriedly into the rice paddies. He wanted to run after his father and ask if he could go along, but Grandmother called to him. "Come here. It's too dangerous out there for you. That mother elephant will be very angry. It's no place for a child."

27

"But, Grandmother," Boonmee protested, "I'm not afraid. I was the one who found him. He's just a baby elephant."

"Your father was right not to take you. Now come here and help me finish this lotus boat," she instructed.

"All right. But, Grandmother, we must give the baby elephant a name. What could we call him?" Boonmee wondered. He thought and thought. Finally he announced his decision. "Since everyone calls him white elephant, that's what I'll name him . . . White Elephant."

His grandmother nodded her approval.

5

Loy Kathong Festival

AS THE MEN approached the wooded area, they became silent. They walked against the wind so that the elephants could not smell them. When they were near the ravine, they could hear the weak, mournful cry of a small elephant and an angry, trumpeted answer from an adult elephant.

The nearer they got to the ravine, the more thrashing they could hear. The men began to walk very slowly and cautiously, their eyes glued to the tree line. It was difficult to guess how many elephants were in there. They decided to stop and discuss ways to get near the ravine safely.

Boonmee's father turned to the village headman and asked, "Why don't we send a couple of men in first to see how many elephants there are? They could climb the same lookout tree that my son used yesterday. Boonmee said he could see most of the ravine from that tall tree on the edge of the tree line."

Heads nodded in agreement. The village headman chose the three youngest men to be scouts. They were all swift runners and could climb the tree faster than anyone else. They each took a torch and a bundle of banana leaves and moved off slowly toward the tree line.

Boonmee's father continued talking to the headman. "We could gather bundles of dried rice stalks to use for fires. Then we could try to separate the big elephants from the little one."

The headman, who had been on several elephant hunts in his life, nodded a knowing "yes." Then he replied, "Let's wait and see how many elephants there are and what the scouts tell us."

Another man suddenly announced, "You know there's a water hole about a mile away. If we waited until the elephants moved off to the water hole, we could set up a circle of fire around the ravine. That would keep them away until we had a chance to dig an incline into the ravine and get the baby elephant out."

Most of the men weren't listening, however. They were watching the three young scouts who were moving closer and closer to the tree line. Suddenly someone shouted, "They're in the tree! They made it!"

The distant trumpeting and thrashing continued while the men watched in silence for a signal from the scouts.

The three scouts in the tree tried to control their heavy breathing as they peered into the ravine. "Sure enough," whispered the youngest scout, "there's a small grayish-white elephant moving around down there." Just then the air was split by a shrieking, spine-tingling trumpet from the mother elephant.

The scouts could see her, too. With huge ears flapping back and forth like giant batwings, she stood at the ravine's edge. In a rocking fashion, she moved back three steps and then quickly forward three steps. Then she threw her huge trunk, which curved like a giant snake, over her massive head and bellowed out her anger. The once-green earth around the ravine was worn to dirt and dust from her angry pacing. Right now she was a killer elephant. Her two companion elephants stood by more calmly, but occasionally they would move to the ravine's edge and trumpet in sympathy.

To the three men in the tree, there seemed to be no way to get to the helpless baby elephant, as long as his furious mother guarded his trap. The men watched, frightened, for almost two hours. Then they decided that two scouts should stay in the tree to keep watch on the white elephant while the third reported back to the headman. The youngest of the three would go back.

When he returned to the waiting men, the scout told the chief about the angry mother elephant and her two companions, and about the very small and frightened white elephant. The village headman thought for a moment. He looked at the sun. "We only have two hours of daylight left. We'd better wait until tomorrow."

"But what about the men in the tree?" asked the young scout.

"You go back out there. The elephants will probably leave for the watering hole in the early hours of dawn. Tell the scouts that they should set fire to their torches then, or if it's daylight, they should burn the banana leaves. The leaves will smolder, making a black smoke. When we see your signal, we'll move in. Some of our men will bring bundles of rice stalks and banana leaves. We'll put up a circle of fire and smoke around the ravine."

The young scout repeated the plan and then headed for the tree line, making certain that he kept moving against the wind. The men decided to post a night watch in the paddies in case the scouts needed help. Not too far to the south, there was a small rain shed made of thatched palms. It would make a good sentinel post for the night.

They decided that two men at a time would take the watch for three hours each. As soon as all the plans were made, two men moved toward the rain shed, picking up dried rice stalks on their way. The other men worked hurriedly in the remaining hour and half of sunlight to tie together bundles of rice stalks for tomorrow's hunt.

While the men were working frantically in the fields, the women of the village were busy preparing food for the Loy Kathong Festival. In Boonmee's house there was great excitement. Even

Grandmother, who was bent and crippled, seemed to move about with more energy. Tonight, there would be the traditional festival fish dish, fried rice, boiled eggs, greens from the *klong*, and coconut sweets.

But when Boonmee's father came home in the last rays of daylight, the evening meal was almost forgotten. His father talked on and on about the white elephant they hoped to capture. But he was also worried for fear the small elephant would hurt himself or become sick from lack of food and water.

"Mother," Boonmee said softly, "he's such a small elephant and he's really scared. He's all alone in that ravine trap."

Father comforted Boonmee and his sisters somewhat by telling them, "If our plans go right, by tomorrow afternoon we should have the white elephant inside the temple compound. He'll be safe there and we can feed and water him."

"Father, I thought the elephant should have a name. I thought about it carefully this afternoon. It seems best to call him White Elephant. What do you think?" asked Boonmee.

Boonmee's father smiled warmly. "That's about the best name for him, I think."

Boonmee picked at his fried rice. He couldn't think about eating right now. "Father, may I go with you tomorrow, please?"

"Son, I'm scheduled for watch at the rain hut from three to six tomorrow morning. You'll be sound asleep when I go out."

"Please, Father, take me with you. I'm not afraid and I'll be very quiet," Boonmee pleaded.

Boonmee's father frowned and shook his head in silence. He had a faraway look in his eyes. Boonmee picked at his rice again. He couldn't eat another grain.

33

The special fish dish went almost untouched. The rice bowl was still almost full when the evening meal was over. No one seemed very hungry. There was too much excitement in the air.

Everyone moved outside to the *klong* to await the festival. The people in the village would float their *kathongs* first, then the people who lived along the *klong* would put theirs out as the village *kathongs* floated by.

Boonmee sat quietly in the darkness of his house. He was troubled. Over and over he wondered to himself, "What will happen if the white elephant dies or is badly hurt when the men try to get him out of the ravine?" Would bad luck come to his village, his father, his family? He wished he knew the answer.

His mother spoke his name softly from the doorway. "Boonmee, come outside. The moon is about to rise. Come, get your lotus boat! It's nearly time for the first *kathongs* to leave the village."

Boonmee stood on the bank, a small, slender silhouette. He stood as Thai children have stood for centuries at the Loy Kathong Festival. When the first sounds of the village musicians' gongs and cymbals floated down the *klong*, Boonmee shivered with excitement.

What should his wish be? For months Boonmee had thought that he would wish to travel to the end of the waterway to see the things Phra Kruu talked about. But now he didn't know what to do. Maybe he should make a wish for the baby elephant's safety.

Boonmee's four sisters chattered noisily and excitedly, but for Boonmee it was a time of silence. He looked about in the shadows for his grandmother. He knew she would have his *kathong,* but he couldn't see her.

Everyone was gay and excited. Tonight was very special. The 34 white elephant would be caught tomorrow . . . if they had luck.

Tonight at the festival many of the wishes would be for success tomorrow.

In the village groups of men, women, girls, and boys danced the traditional Thai dance. Moving in two circles, the men and women, each in a different circle, twisted and turned in step to the

musicians' gongs and cymbals. Their outstretched fingers moved like the classic dancers of old, telling of happiness tonight. Their dancing shadows played on the ground like shadow puppets. Small children holding their *kathongs* watched excitedly as the adults sang and danced happiness into the darkening night.

Phra Kruu, his orange robes picking up the flickering fires from the torches, walked slowly down the street like a golden Buddha. The village headman walked proudly by his side. People with *kathongs*, torches, and musical instruments fell in behind them. They were heading for the water's edge. It was time to send their offerings and wishes to the Mother-of-the-Waters by floating the *kathongs* to her.

Suddenly Boonmee's oldest sister screamed, "There's one! There's one!" From the darkness near the village came a sputter of light. It was brief but clear, pinpointing a hole in the darkness, as has happened throughout the ages. It was the first lotus boat from the village. The festival was under way.

A tingle of excitement surged through Boonmee's body. This was the night he had waited for so long. But now he didn't know what to do. Where was his grandmother? Where was his *kathong*? He turned toward his house and saw the bent figure of his grandmother coming to the *klong*.

"Grandmother, where have you been? The first *kathongs* have already left the village," said Boonmee as he took his *kathong* from his grandmother's gnarled hand.

"I was at the spirit house, Boonmee. Can you hear the music yet?" she asked in an excited whisper.

"Yes, Grandmother. And the first *kathong* is coming now."

"Boonmee, I don't see so good anymore. Tell me what you see," she said as she moved closer to him.

"I can see two candle flames winking in the distance. They're close together like the eyes of a giant cat. Those cat eyes seem to be skimming over the water. It's like magic, Grandmother," said Boonmee.

"Now, I can see more candle flames. There are hundreds of them! They are like shimmering slivers . . . like cat's whiskers. Grandmother, it looks like a giant Siamese cat and it's floating down the *klong* toward us! Grandmother, it's beautiful." Boonmee's voice trailed off. He stood silently, watching the *kathongs*, aglow with candles, as they drifted toward him. He didn't notice his grandmother walk away.

Behind the glimmering *kathongs* came wooden boats that carried the musicians. The boats with their torches seemed to be chasing the giant cat. Flickering skyward like the pointed tongues of snakes, the torches from the musicians' boats lit a path for the singing villagers who followed in their own boats. The haunting tones of reed pipes floated lightly in the night air as the gongs and cymbals marked out the forward strokes of the oarsmen.

As the first two lotus boats floated past the neighboring houses, Boonmee could see the candle lights of the *kathongs* that moved from the banks to merge with what looked like the shimmering body of a giant cat.

As the procession came closer, Boonmee's sisters lit the candles in their *kathongs*. The light from the candles glowed in their faces. Their straight black hair hung down like dark veils to protect their eyes from the candles' brightness. Together they stood like four statues, waiting to come to life.

When the first *kathongs* from the village passed them, they bent down to the water's edge and slipped their precious lotus boats into the dark waters. Each held her *kathong* for a brief moment to make her wish, then gently small brown fingers released the lotus boat. Each *kathong* carried a flickering candle, a smoldering incense stick, and a private wish.

Still squatting, the little girls watched their tiny lotus boats bob and weave. Each tried to take its place in the stream of glittering candles. Two of them struck out courageously, but a third bobbed, sputtered, dipped, and then went out. Boonmee's youngest sister broke into tears.

The fourth *kathong* caught on some reeds. It burned brightly, but it didn't move. Boonmee's oldest sister cautiously splashed her hands in the dark water to make waves. Finally her splashing freed the small lotus boat, causing it to dance and twirl about in the water. Suddenly it broke away and headed out to the main current. Boonmee's sister giggled with delight.

Boonmee sank to the ground. Staring at the *klong* all aglow like a star-sprinkled heaven, he thought of Phra Kruu. What would Phra Kruu want him to do? Should he make a wish for himself or for the struggling baby elephant?

The musicians floated by. Singing villagers called out greetings to his family as they drifted past. Village boats darted carefully around the flickering *kathongs*. The music and songs became faint. Some candles were still bobbing courageously in the dark waters, but many *kathongs* would never make it to the Mother-of-theWaters.

Tenderly Boonmee took out his match and lit the candle. He held his pink lotus boat to the moon. It was beautiful and strong, and it would travel a long way. Boonmee knew what he would wish. He knew what he had to wish.

The white candle glowed brightly, turning his *kathong* into

a silver vessel, beautiful enough for Lord Buddha. He waded out into the waters. For a moment he held it between his hands in the gesture of an offering. He bowed his head and made his wish.

"I wish," he began slowly, "that my father and his friends will capture the elephant safely. I wish that no harm will come to the little white elephant. I wish that my old grandmother may see the King and Queen before she dies and I wish. . . ." Boonmee stopped. He stood motionless for a moment, looking up at the moon. "That's all I wish." With both hands holding his *kathong*, he slipped it into the water.

His candle was so bright that it was easy to follow. Straight and strong, it floated away. It seemed to move faster than the others, floating past several of the lagging ones. It darted around a couple of sputtering *kathongs* like a warrior heading into battle. Soon, like the first *kathong* of the evening, it became only a pinpoint in the darkness.

He waded ashore looking for his grandmother to tell her that he had changed his wish, but she was gone. No one remained on the bank. Farther down the *klong*, he saw someone strike a match. In the momentary flare he recognized his grandmother's face, and he raced down the bank toward her.

Intent with her thoughts, she was bending low over a small candle. Boonmee stopped to watch. In her gnarled hands, she tenderly held a small and ragged-looking lotus boat. It wasn't really a *kathong* at all. It wasn't neatly woven like the one she helped him make, but was lopsided and funny looking.

With great difficulty, she bent down to the water's edge. "Oh, Mother-of-the-Waters, this is my last wish in this life. Give happiness and good fortune to my grandson. He's a good boy." With a groan, she set her sad *kathong* afloat.

She got up painfully and started up the bank to where Boonmee stood. "Oh, Boon, I didn't know you were here! You startled me!" she said hoarsely, with a tinge of anger in her voice.

Tears came to Boonmee's eyes. He looked down at his old grandmother climbing up the bank. Then he looked at the *kathong* on the water. It was small and flickering . . . the very last one.

"Grandmother, where did you get that *kathong*?" Boonmee asked gently.

"Somehow tonight I felt you would change your wish. You would wish for the white elephant and not for yourself," she said.

"That's right, Grandmother. How did you know?" he asked.

"I knew. So I decided to make a wish for you. When I went to the spirit house, I tried to make a *kathong*. I'm afraid it wasn't beautiful, but maybe it will make it," she remarked softly. "Is it still floating?" she asked.

Boonmee looked into the darkness. He wasn't certain. There was a tiny, very dim flickering that came and went. Maybe it was his grandmother's wish. Yes, it must be!

"Yes, I see it, Grandmother! I see it! It's beautiful! Thank you." He put his arm around his grandmother and they walked back to the house in the silence of darkness.

As they approached the house, Boonmee could hear his mother and father talking. They were sitting on the steps in the darkness waiting for Boonmee and his grandmother to return.

"Son," his father began, "do you still want to go with me for the three o'clock watch?"

"Oh, yes, Father, yes!" Boonmee answered quickly.

"Well, then, get some sleep. I'll wake you when it's time to go," announced his father.

"Thank you," answered Boonmee. "Thank you."

Boonmee crawled under his white cocoon of mosquito netting. He was very tired. He closed his eyes and saw again the sparkling candles flickering into shapes of giant cats. Then they diminished into a single candle light that illuminated the wrinkled and toothless face of his dear, old grandmother.

The Loy Kathong Festival had ended.

6

Capturing the White Elephant

"HURRY," urged Boonmee's father. "We mustn't keep the other men waiting." Boonmee, trying to walk faster, stumbled. Something cut into his bare foot, but he said nothing.

His father called out a greeting to the two men sitting in front of the rain hut. "What's happened tonight?" he asked them.

"Nothing yet. The mother elephant is still there. She's trumpeting and walking guard. You'll hear her," said one of his father's friends.

"What happened to the other two big elephants?" Father asked quickly.

"They left just as the sun was setting last night and haven't returned. They have probably abandoned the mother elephant and gone back to the herd."

"Great news! Now you two go on home," announced his

father, as he motioned for Boonmee to sit down in the corner of the hut. "Boonmee and I will keep guard, and the other guard will be coming soon."

Boonmee nestled into a corner. The night was quiet, but there was a feeling of mystery. He leaned his head back against the wall to rest and think. Soon he fell asleep.

When he heard the men talking excitedly outside the hut, Boonmee jumped to his feet and scampered out, trying to shake the sleep from his eyes. In the distance spurts of flaming torches licked into the dim light of dawn. Boonmee's father turned to him. "Son, she's gone. There's the signal. The mother elephant has probably headed out for the water hole!"

Boonmee wrapped his arms around himself to protect his body from the morning chill. They all stood watching the flaming treetop. This was what they had been waiting for. With the mother elephant gone, they could circle the ravine with fire to keep her away. Then they could capture the little white elephant.

Boonmee looked up anxiously at the faces of the two men. What would they do now? How long would the mother elephant be gone?

"We must get help from the village quickly!" announced the other man. "We have to get the baby elephant out before she gets back."

Boonmee's father looked down at his son standing straight and tall by his side. "Boonmee, you must run to the village. Go tell Phra Kruu. He will ring the temple gong to wake the men. We have to get the dried bundles of rice stalks and the banana leaves into a circle around the white elephant to keep his angry mother away. Hurry now! Hurry, son!"

Boonmee took off running. His bare feet flew through the   *45* stubbles in the rice paddies, and he leaped over the small irrigation ditches. He put his head down and ran like a warrior of old even though his legs ached, his mouth was dry, and he felt stabbing pains in his chest. He knew he must get the men back to help his father and the scouts before the mother elephant returned.

As the soft, tropical morning light gave shadows to the world of darkness, the small Thai boy raced with his whole heart across the Thai countryside. Past the darkened village houses, he sped. He could see the temple outline against the lightening sky. As he neared the temple compound, he heard the reassuring sound of the temple wind-chimes over the sound of his heavy breathing.

The monks were already awake in the temple. Boonmee ran straight to Phra Kruu's room just as Phra Kruu was coming out his door.

"Phra Kruu! Phra Kruu!" screamed Boonmee, quickly putting his small hands to his face to greet the monk. "The mother elephant has gone! Hit the gong! Hit the gong!"

Without a word, Phra Kruu raced to the platform, picked up a wooden mallet, and struck the huge, round gong. *Booooong! Booooong! Booooong!* The alarm rang through the village. Men came running from the dark houses, picking up their waiting bundles of banana leaves and coils of ropes.

Still banging the gong, Phra Kruu leaned over to the breathless Boonmee. "Why were you out there, Boonmee?"

Between gasps, Boonmee replied, "My father said that I could go with him on the morning watch."

The compound filled with excited men. Already the village headman was leading the way out of the village. Villagers fell in behind him.

46

Phra Kruu turned to follow the men, then looked back at Boonmee, whose big brown eyes pleaded silently. "Please let me come," he said, "I found the elephant. He's mine."

"All right, you can come, Boonmee." Phra Kruu reached for the boy's hand.

Out near the ravine, two of the scouts had come to help Boonmee's father and the other man. Before the scouts could ask what to do, Boonmee's father shouted to them. "Start carrying those bundles of rice stalks to the ravine. Carry as many as you can and put them in a large circle around the ravine."

The mother elephant had wandered slowly down to the water hole about a mile away. She was thirsty and tired from her long watch at the ravine. The scout in the treetop could see her as she lumbered farther and farther into the distance.

When the villagers saw the dark figures of their friends scurrying about in the field ahead, they broke into a run. The village headman shouted orders while they ran. "Pick up the rice bundles. Head for the ravine. Make a circle. You two men get the torches ready. Quick, everyone! We don't have much time!"

In the calmness of the Thai dawn, the mother elephant played in the cooling water, unaware of the men surrounding her baby.

The men worked feverishly laying rice stalks and bundles of banana leaves around the ravine. The heavy elephants had already trampled the vegetation, so it was easy for the men to prepare the circle.

The scout in the tree watched carefully for the return of the mother elephant, but there was no sign of her. The small elephant threw himself against the steep sides of the ravine in vain attempts to get out.

48

Boonmee's father and four other men dug furiously at one end of the ravine to make an incline so they could pull out the white elephant. It was hard work because the mother elephant had stamped down the dirt until it was as solid as cement.

Boonmee watched in silence from behind Phra Kruu's robes. Then he saw an idle pick and decided that he would help, too. He grabbed the pick and started hacking away at the packed earth. In the excitement, his father didn't notice him. The morning sun hung low over the eastern horizon like a huge warning sign. Time was passing quickly. The men knew they must hurry.

"Ready!" shouted one of the men. "The incline is finished. Get the ropes!"

Several men on both sides of the ravine grabbed ropes and threw them at the frightened elephant's feet. With each heave, the men shouted. With each miss, they moaned.

The baby elephant, panicked by the men's shouts, raced from one end of the ravine to the other. In desperation, he put up his small trunk and trumpeted a miserable cry. Once, twice, three times, he trumpeted for help.

The ropes fell useless. In his frantic race to escape, the little elephant was too quick for them. The men couldn't catch his running legs as they had hoped.

He stopped for a moment. His floppy ears hung sadly. He was breathing hard. He raised his head to look at the creatures who were making so much noise at the sides of the ravine. When he looked in Boonmee's direction, Boonmee shuddered. For a brief instant, he looked at the frightened elephant's eyes.

"He wants me to help him," thought Boonmee.

"She's coming! She's coming! She's running!" shrieked a voice

49

from the treetop. The mother elephant had heard her baby's cry for help. She was coming on the run.

The men dropped their ropes and headed for the circle of rice stalks and banana leaves. The village headman shouted, "Don't light them until I tell you. Then start shouting. Make all the noise you can!"

Boonmee looked down into the ravine. The small white elephant stood helplessly. His sides pumped in and out rapidly. He watched Boonmee with sad and frightened eyes.

A loud trumpeting pierced the air. The mother elephant was near. Then her thumping-running pace shook the ground. "She's close!" shouted the treetop scout.

"Now!" yelled the village headman. "Now!"

Torches ignited in a blaze of heat. The men moved forward with their giant matches. *Whoooosh!* The rice stalks roared into mighty fires. Tremendous heat surged from the fiery circle.

"She stopped! But she's mad. She's digging up the ground and the bushes with her feet. I think she's going to charge!" shouted the voice from the tree.

"Set fire to the banana leaves," ordered the village headman. The men pitched their torches on the bundles of banana leaves that were lumped between the blazing piles of rice stalks. Thick, heavy, black smoke rose chokingly from the green bundles. That would keep her away . . . maybe.

While the men shouted and kept the circle of fire ablaze, Boonmee took two ropes and slid down the newly dug incline into the ravine with the white elephant.

The little elephant stood rigidly, just watching. He didn't flinch. Boonmee began speaking softly to the frightened elephant. As

51

he spoke, he inched his way toward the sad-eyed creature. Closer and closer he moved. The little elephant watched him suspiciously, but he didn't retreat.

Phra Kruu saw what Boonmee was doing and edged to the rim of the ravine to watch.

With one hand extended in friendship, Boonmee used his free hand to maneuver a rope. He talked kindly to the elephant. "Don't move, little one. I won't hurt you. You're a lucky elephant. No harm will come to you."

The white elephant retreated a few steps. His eyes reflected panic. His gaze never wandered from the small boy.

"I found you," Boonmee whispered as he drew nearer. "I'll take care of you. I'll get you out of here. Stand still, little one."

Slowly, ever so slowly, he bent down before the wheezing elephant. Cautiously he put one rope around his own neck for later use. With both hands he reached out and roped the elephant's right front leg and hurriedly tied a knot. Boonmee was excited, but he tried not to show it. He didn't want to frighten the elephant.

With great care, he stood up. He glanced at the ravine's edge for help. There stood Phra Kruu. Phra Kruu motioned for him to toss him the loose end of the rope. Still uttering gentle sounds to the elephant, he backed away with the rope in his hands.

Phra Kruu, who was now kneeling, extended his arm down into the ravine. With one eye on the elephant and the other searching for Phra Kruu's hand, Boonmee tossed the loose end of the rope to the monk.

Phra Kruu caught it and ran to the nearest tree to wrap the rope around the trunk.

52   Boonmee took the second rope from around his neck. He must

dare to get the other rope around the elephant's left leg. Like a brave warrior, he inched slowly, barely moving, toward the elephant. This time, the elephant stepped back farther. The rope on his right foot grew taut! "Oh! I hope the rope doesn't hurt him. It will frighten him," thought Boonmee.

Once again he extended his slender brown arm. "Please stand still, little friend. Don't move. Let me get closer. Do you know that I've given you a name? It's White Elephant . . . White Elephant. Do you like it?"

The baby elephant seemed to be hypnotized by this small creature who spoke so softly to him. His sad elephant eyes watched Boonmee's every move.

"She's charging! She's charging!" A great roar went up. Torches waved frantically in the air. Men screamed and yelled, trying to frighten the mother elephant away. She suddenly stopped. She trumpeted wildly, then retreated. She stood outside the circle of fire helplessly.

White Elephant's small grayish-white trunk went up, and he responded to all the noise with a weak cry.

Boonmee stood motionless, but he continued to talk to his newly acquired friend. When the little elephant seemed more quiet, Boonmee began to walk toward him again. Carefully he moved in close to put the rope around the elephant's left leg. Success! He made it! He had him!

Boonmee again searched the ravine's edge for assistance. By this time Phra Kruu had ordered several men to the other side of the ravine to wait for the second rope. They were to hold the rope tightly in case the little elephant tried to get away. Skillfully Boonmee tossed the second rope to the waiting men.

"She's retreating! She's still mad, but she's leaving!" yelled the scout.

Boonmee's father hurried back to the ravine, still carrying his burning torch. He stopped at the ravine's edge. He couldn't believe what he saw.

Boonmee stood in front of White Elephant. White Elephant was extending his crinkly trunk out to Boonmee. It was quivering. Boonmee kept his hand out in friendship as he explained to the little elephant that it was all right.

The moist pink end of his trunk touched Boonmee's hand.

He jerked it back in fright! But Boonmee kept his hand out. More and more men came to the ravine's edge to see the miracle of Boonmee and the lucky white elephant.

White Elephant hesitated for a few moments. His trunk quivered out to meet Boonmee's waiting hand. This time he didn't jerk it back. Boonmee took a couple of steps backwards toward the incline. The baby elephant, with his small trunk nuzzling Boonmee's hand, followed.

The rope that Phra Kruu had tied about the tree trunk was now being held by six husky men. The rope men on both sides held the ropes taut, but not so tight as to frighten the baby elephant.

The only noise now was the crackling of the burning fires and the hushed child's voice talking to the gray-white elephant. The men stood in silence and disbelief.

Miraculously, the small Thai boy enticed the baby elephant to the incline. The little elephant licked the salty perspiration from Boonmee's skin. His trunk moved from Boonmee's hand up along his arm in a nuzzling fashion. White Elephant was following him.

They reached the incline. White Elephant's round foot plopped to rest on the rising earth of the incline. He stopped. Boonmee continued backwards. But the elephant didn't move. He just leaned and stretched, trying to keep his wet trunk on Boonmee. He hesitated, took one step, then another.

First came Boonmee over the edge of the ravine's incline, then came the pinkness of the elephant's trunk, then the little elephant's head. A few more steps and he would be out.

The men holding the ropes stood tense and ready. Now they could pull the elephant out of the ravine if necessary. The village headman calmly ordered, "Those fires may scare him. Be ready to wrap the ropes tightly around the trees to hold him."

Two quick steps and the little elephant was out of the ravine. He was free! Now he belonged to the Thai Kingdom.

The elephant looked much smaller now. He just stood at the ravine's brink and looked around. Then his trunk went back to Boonmee. This time he moved it up and down Boonmee's face while Boonmee stood proudly and smiled. This was really his elephant. He was kissing him.

The long trip from the foothills to the village had exhausted the baby elephant and he soon fell asleep in a corner of the temple compound. After he had consumed lots of water and food, the monks' helpers had washed the dirt off. Then he slept.

A few inches from the white elephant, a small boy lay on a straw mat. His entire body, except his head and one arm, was covered with a piece of cloth. Boonmee had begged Phra Kruu to let him sleep in the temple compound by the elephant. Now he lay asleep with his brown arm reaching out to touch the small elephant's trunk.

Men, in groups of three, were posted at various points around the village to watch for the angry mother elephant who might attack the village in revenge. The men carried torches and kerosene. If she came, they would drive her away with fire. All night long the weary men peered into the country darkness, but she never came. Twice they heard a forlorn trumpet in the distance. They thought it might be the sad mother searching for her lost baby, but they never caught sight of her. The little white elephant's mother would never know that her baby was destined for greatness.

White Elephant and Boonmee slept soundly. The wind-chimes atop the temple tinkled soft, sleepy tunes. All seemed safe in the small Thai village. In Boonmee's house, his grandmother slept peacefully. She was happy for she knew her wish would come true.

7

The Coming of the
King and Queen

EVERY morning after breakfast, Boonmee would run to the temple to be with his elephant. He had stayed with White Elephant for the first two nights, but then his father had insisted that he come home. There was work to be done.

The small elephant was no longer tied to a tree in the corner of the compound. He roamed about freely. After each day's scrubbing, he became whiter and whiter, but he was still a grayish-white.

The baby elephant no longer cried for his mother. He would eat from the hands of the temple assistants, but he liked it best when Boonmee fed him. Whenever Boonmee entered the compound, the little elephant's trunk would go up and he would begin to sniff. Then he would come to Boonmee, his small pink nuzzle quivering with excitement.

His greeting to Boonmee was the same every morning. First he nuzzled the boy's outstretched hand. Then he nibbled his trunk up Boonmee's arm to his face. Very carefully his soft trunk nibbled at Boonmee's face, giving him wet elephant kisses.

These were happy and busy days for Boonmee and for the people of his village. Plans were under way for the ceremony where the white elephant would be given to the King, but Boonmee paid little attention to the plans. He was interested only in keeping his little friend as long as possible.

Then one morning as Boonmee was feeding the elephant, Phra Kruu came over to him and said, "Boonmee, tomorrow afternoon they will take the elephant away."

Boonmee was horrified. "No, not yet. He's still just a baby!"

"It's all been arranged with the government officials. The village men will lead the elephant out to the main road where one of the government trucks will pick him up to carry him to the provincial capital."

"Can I go too?" Boonmee begged.

"I doubt it," answered Phra Kruu. "This is government business."

Boonmee's heart sank. They would take away his baby elephant. So soon! He had been his for only three weeks.

"Oh, please, Phra Kruu. I have to go. He'll be frightened without me," said Boonmee, rubbing behind the elephant's floppy ears.

"I doubt that you can go, but you can certainly attend the ceremonies on Sunday. The whole village will be there," Phra Kruu said, putting a protecting arm around Boonmee.

Boonmee knelt down by his elephant and held the small trunk in his hands. "I'll miss you, little elephant." Tears rolled down Boonmee's face. The little elephant moved his trunk to the boy's face as if to wipe the tears away.

Boonmee looked up at the sad eyes of his elephant friend and smiled at the elephant's wiping his tears. "You are a smart elephant. The legend is true. White elephants are very special."

The next afternoon, village men came with ropes and chains. Boonmee talked softly to the elephant, telling him not to be afraid. "The men will treat you kindly. Be a good elephant."

Quickly the men fastened ropes to his two front legs. The little elephant stood bewildered when they started tugging on him. He froze in fright. The men tugged on the ropes, but they didn't succeed in getting White Elephant to walk. They just pulled his front feet out in front of him, and the little elephant almost lost his balance. He trumpeted in alarm.

Boonmee couldn't watch the men tug and pull on his frightened friend, so he ran to his side. He began talking softly to him and held out his hand. The little pink nuzzle of a trunk came out to his hand in a friendly greeting. Boonmee started walking backwards and his faithful little friend followed.

Slowly they moved out of the temple gates. The men walked beside the elephant, holding ropes that they didn't need now. They moved down the main street of the village, heading for the trail that led to the main road. The little elephant put his trunk on Boonmee's shoulder and walked after him.

The government truck was waiting on the main road. One of the drivers announced their arrival. "Here they come. Hey, look! There's a little boy leading the elephant!"

All the men climbed on top of the truck to see this unusual

sight. They were prepared for the worst and had expected to see the villagers bringing in a fighting, trumpeting elephant that would refuse to get into the truck.

When Boonmee saw the waiting truck, he slowed down. A big lump came into his throat and tears swelled in his eyes. He could feel the softness of the trunk on the back of his neck. He didn't want the men to take his elephant away. White Elephant would be lonely and afraid, as he had been in the ravine.

The men put down boards leading into the back of the truck, and Boonmee slowly walked up the ramp. White Elephant followed, and was loaded painlessly on the truck. Then the driver hollered at Boonmee, "Get out of the truck! We're in a hurry!"

Boonmee threw his arms around the little elephant's head. With tears flowing down his cheeks, he talked into the elephant's big ear. "I love you, little elephant. I'll miss you."

The little elephant wrapped his trunk around Boonmee's waist and pulled him closer. The men became silent. There was softness in their hearts for the small Thai boy and his baby elephant.

Everyone watched in silence. Finally Phra Kruu came to the truck and softly called to Boonmee, "Come, son. The men must go. We'll see him on Sunday. Come with me."

Boonmee gave him one last hug. The little elephant slowly released his friend from the grasp of his trunk. Boonmee jumped over the side of the truck and ran. He ran and ran and ran . . . tears blinding him. He didn't care where he went. He just ran.

That evening he squatted beside his grandmother. She was trying to explain to Boonmee that the white elephant belonged to the people of Thailand. "The elephant will be given to the King in trust for all the people of the Thai nation," said Grandmother, who knew of her grandson's deep sadness.

"Will anyone talk to him and wash him like I did?" asked Boonmee.

"The King's servants will take good care of him. Don't worry, Boonmee. He's a lucky elephant. No harm will come to him. He'll bring luck to all of us. Be happy, my son, that you found him."

Boonmee looked at his grandmother as she spoke. She had tears in her eyes. "Grandmother, why are you crying?"

"I'm crying because I'm happy, Boonmee. This is a happy time for everyone in our family, in our village, and in our country."

Boonmee wondered about that. He wasn't happy like his grandmother. He had been crying, but not because he was happy. He was heartbroken.

As darkness came, the two sat in silence, watching the shadows grow dimmer, until the whole world seemed to be just a shadow. As he stared into the shadows, he could almost see elephants moving about. Sunday seemed such a long time away.

But finally Sunday came. This was the day the King and Queen were to accept the white elephant. Boonmee and his family had been awake long before sunrise. They had to leave early to walk to the main road where they would catch the bus to the provincial capital.

The day was hot, and the bus was crowded. To Boonmee the orange and blue bus seemed to crawl like a pokey caterpillar. He wished the bus would hurry. He was on his way to see his elephant.

Boonmee had never been to the provincial capital. It was a big city, or at least Boonmee thought so, crowded with people. There were buses, bicycles, *samlars*, and many stores. But it was easy to find the ceremonial grounds. That's where all the people were heading. Music and laughter filled the air.

As they pushed their way through the crowds, Boonmee held his grandmother's arm. His eyes were searching the area for his beloved white elephant.

"Grandmother, can you see the elephant? There are too many people in the way and I can't see over them," Boonmee said, making little kangaroo jumps to try to see over the heads of the adults.

"I can't see him, Boonmee, but I don't see so good," his grandmother replied.

Inside the ceremonial grounds, Boonmee's father went to the village headman. "Where will the people from our village sit?" he inquired.

"Right here in the middle, in front of the King's platform," replied the headman.

"Right in front of the King?" questioned his grandmother.

"Well, almost in front. Some other people are sitting in the first five rows . . . government officials, important people," added the headman.

The headman led them to the seats reserved for his village people. Before Boonmee got settled on his bench, he cried out, "Look! Look over there! There's my white elephant!"

Standing regal in the shade of several giant palm trees, the baby elephant looked about inquisitively. He was wearing the bright red and silver cloth that had been made by the women of Boonmee's village. He looked like a royal elephant already. But he was a very small royal elephant.

As fast as a frightened tadpole, Boonmee was gone. As he approached the elephant, he slowed down because he didn't want to scare him. He held out his hand, talking softly. "Little elephant, it's me, Boonmee."

The elephant's head moved toward Boonmee and his trunk went out. It twitched in the air. Then he recognized Boonmee's smell and came to him.

"You remember me! You remember me!" cried Boonmee, joyously.

Passers-by stopped to look at the little white elephant giving wet elephant kisses to a small Thai boy. Soon Boonmee and White Elephant were in an embrace. Boonmee put his arms around the elephant's head and talked into his big, floppy ear. The baby elephant wrapped his trunk around the boy's waist, as he had done on the day they parted.

"I missed you, little elephant," Boonmee whispered in his ear.

A crowd gathered to watch Boonmee and the elephant.

Proudly the village headman arrived to announce to all the onlookers that this boy was from his village, and he was the one who had found the white elephant.

Thai music floated across the crowd mixing with the laughter and gaiety everywhere. This was a great day for the people. They would be visited by their King and Queen, and they would give to the nation one of the greatest symbols of good fortune . . . a white elephant.

But to Boonmee the day was both happy and sad. Today his grandmother would see the King and Queen and his nation would be given good luck. But also today he would lose his little white elephant forever!

Finally Boonmee's father came to get him. "Boonmee, you must leave the elephant now. He belongs to the Kingdom. Come back and sit with us. The King and Queen will be here soon," explained his father.

Sadly Boonmee backed away from his friend. "I'll be back to see you before I leave."

Boonmee joined his family, sitting between his grandmother and his mother. It was very hot now and his grandmother was feeling dizzy. She had been in the sun for over two hours, but she didn't mind too much. She had waited all her life to see the King and Queen.

"How much longer do we have to wait?" pleaded Boonmee.

"They'll be here soon, Boonmee, soon," replied his mother, wiping perspiration from her face.

Boonmee could see White Elephant if he ducked and bobbed between heads. Suddenly a hush fell over the crowd. Music interrupted the hush, and the inspirational Thai National Anthem seemed to push away the afternoon heat. Everyone stood in silence. Boonmee couldn't see anything, but he stood in obedience. His heart beat rapidly. The King and Queen had arrived.

The entire crowd turned in the direction of the approaching royalty. The villagers *whai*ed. With their hands prayer-like before their faces, they fell to their knees in respect as the King and Queen marched through the aisle of royal soldiers.

Boonmee knew he should not raise his eyes as they passed, so he glanced at his grandmother's folded hands. They were shaking and they were covered with tears.

The King and Queen regally climbed the steps to the royal platform. They were protected from the searing sun by two huge golden umbrellas that glittered and sparkled. Each umbrella was carried by a man dressed in a red uniform of old. The King and Queen sat down on two jeweled throne chairs in the center of the platform. When they were seated, all the people sat down.

Boonmee's eyes grew large as he looked at his King and Queen   *67*

for the first time. The Queen was as beautiful as Sita, the goddess of the legends. Her emerald-green silk gown glittered with golden threads. It was long and graceful. Her black hair was pulled back from her face, forming a bundle of curls at the back of her head. Her face seemed whiter than the faces of the village women. It was like ivory. She was, indeed, a Queen.

The Governor, in a military-style uniform, was talking over a loud speaker, but Boonmee wasn't listening. He was completely awed by the royal couple. The King, in a white uniform, sat stately and stiff. Rows of colorful medals hung from his jacket. He wore dark sunglasses. His face was handsome, but solemn.

"He looks like he doesn't smile often," thought Boonmee. "It probably isn't any fun to be King."

"To His Majesty, King Bhumipol, and to all the people of Thailand, we humbly give the traditional symbol of good fortune— a white elephant," the military-looking Governor announced.

As he spoke, four Thai Army Officers led the little elephant to the front of the King's platform. The officers stood at attention. White Elephant tilted his head to one side as if to get a better look at the King and Queen.

The handsome King began to speak. "People of Thailand, this is a most auspicious day for our nation. The white elephant should bring us good fortune in the days and years ahead. It is a good sign for all of us."

He spoke gently. Boonmee, listening carefully, reconsidered. "Maybe the King doesn't smile because he is concerned about the people of his Kingdom," he thought.

Boonmee looked up at his grandmother's face. She was squinting, and she held her hands to her eyes to protect them from the sun. *69*

"Grandmother, can you see?" whispered Boonmee, tugging at her skirt.

In reverent silence, she shook her head, no. A sickening pain stabbed Boonmee's heart. She had waited all these years to see the King and now it was too late. Her old, worn-out eyes couldn't see that far. She probably couldn't hear what the King was saying, either, her hearing was so poor.

"The elephant will be placed inside the Palace Grounds in Bangkok. It will grow and live a long life, bringing good fortune to all . . . especially to the people who caught the white elephant and who now offer him to the nation," continued the King.

Suddenly the King turned to the Governor and said, "I understand that a young boy was responsible for finding this lucky elephant."

The Governor bowed and replied, "Yes, Your Majesty. A boy by the name of Boonmee Booserwongse."

"Is that boy here today?" asked the King.

The Governor looked at the village headman who nodded his head. "Yes, Your Majesty, he's here," answered the Governor.

Boonmee's heart was pounding in his chest, in his head, in his legs, in his arms. They were saying his name . . . his name . . . Boonmee Booserwongse. He was scared.

"Will Boonmee Booserwongse come forward?" asked the King quietly.

Boonmee grabbed his grandmother's hand. "What's wrong?" she whispered, not being able to hear the King's words.

"Grandmother, the King wants me to come up on the platform with him," choked Boonmee.

70   Grandmother grabbed both his hands in hers and squeezed.

Gently his mother put her arm around his shaking body. "Go, Boonmee. The King is calling you."

"Will Boonmee please come to the platform." The Governor's voice rang out in a sing-song fashion like a temple gong.

His small legs would hardly move. He was scared—more scared than the day he found the white elephant. The King was calling him! It seemed such a long way to the ceremonial platform. Boonmee was shaking all over. He squeezed past the villagers in his row, heading for the platform.

As he passed the white elephant, the pink nuzzle of the little elephant's trunk went out to sniff and caught Boonmee's scent as he walked by. The little elephant gave a carefree toss of his trunk and marched after Boonmee.

Boonmee didn't know that the little elephant was following him until he heard the King say, "Boonmee, it seems you have a friend walking behind you."

Boonmee turned so suddenly that the little elephant's out-stretched trunk came right into Boonmee's face.

"No, little elephant! No! You must stay with the army officers," said Boonmee, who was embarrassed that the King's elephant was following him rather than staying with the King's guards. The little elephant gave Boonmee his warm and wet elephant kisses while Boonmee talked softly to him until the army men came to take him back.

Boonmee walked as straight, tall, and stiff as his shaking body would allow. Up the stairs, across the platform he went. It didn't seem like he had any legs. But somehow, he managed to kneel before his King.

The young Thai King looked down at the small boy kneeling

before him. The King could tell that Boonmee was frightened. "Boon-mee, it looks like you did more than capture our Kingdom's first white elephant in many years. You have also made friends with him."

Boonmee couldn't answer. He could only nod his head, yes, and bow his head lower in respect. He was too scared to say anything.

"I'm proud of you, Boonmee, for your bravery in capturing the white elephant. You are a good example of the bravery and courage of our young Thai people," the King proclaimed.

Goose bumps chased up and down Boonmee's body when the King talked so nicely about him. His grandmother would be proud.

The King seemed to be finished talking, so Boonmee glanced up at the beautiful Queen Sirikrit and bowed low before Her Majesty. As Boonmee was standing up to leave, he noticed that the lovely Queen was smiling at him. A tingle ran through his small body.

Boonmee backed away politely from the royal couple. Then he quickly scampered down the steps and back to the safety of his family. He was almost in tears by the time he reached them. His mother put comforting arms around her trembling son.

White Elephant was taken back to the shade of the banana trees, and the ceremony continued. Important officials spoke. Then there was folk-dancing for the King and Queen. During the dancing, Boonmee slipped away from the crowd and edged his way to the giant banana trees. He had to say goodbye to his beloved little elephant.

As usual the elephant smelled him coming and stretched out a wet trunk in greeting. They almost seemed to be talking together. The elephant followed all of Boonmee's movements with his eyes and trunk. They were in a world apart . . . the little gray-white elephant and the nut-brown boy.

72   With music still playing, the King and Queen left the royal

platform to return to their waiting limousine for the long trip back to Bangkok. Boonmee was so involved with his elephant that he didn't even know the King and Queen were leaving.

As the King began to descend the steps, his eyes caught sight of the white elephant with his trunk around Boonmee. The King watched for a brief moment and then turned to whisper something to the Governor.

The King and the Governor walked toward Boonmee and the lucky elephant. The King didn't say a word. He watched and listened.

"Be a good elephant," whispered Boonmee. "Bring lots of good luck to our country. You were the nicest friend I ever had. I'll miss you so much."

The little elephant, somehow understanding the tenderness in his little friend's words, wrapped his trunk around Boonmee's waist and pulled him close. Tears rolled down Boonmee's face. "I must go now, little one. I'll remember you always. Be good."

The King was touched by the small boy's love for the elephant. "Boonmee, you have brought good luck to our country and happiness to your village," he said quietly. "I want to thank you. What can I do for you?"

Boonmee bowed low before looking up at the King. He thought carefully, and then replied, "Your Majesty, my grandmother has wanted to see the King all her life. She is very old and cannot see or hear well. She's here today, but she couldn't see you because she was too far away. Could I bring her here to see you?"

"Yes, Boonmee, bring her here," answered the King.

Boonmee, his eyes afire with excitement, looked at the huge crowd of people. How could he find his grandmother among all the people? He must find her quickly or the King would be gone.

73

He dashed and darted among the people, trying to find the bench where he had left his family. Finally he recognized his mother's purple blouse and scrambled through the crowd toward her.

"Mother, Mother!" he cried. "I'm going to take Grandmother to see the King. He said I could!"

His mother couldn't believe what her son was saying. She just stared at him. Boonmee looked at his old grandmother's wrinkled and withered face. "Grandmother, come with me to meet the King!" said Boonmee, taking her hand.

A faraway look came into her tired eyes, and tears welled up in them. She didn't utter a word, but just followed Boonmee, holding tight to his little hand.

The soldiers who were in a circle around the King opened a path for Boonmee and his grandmother. Inside the circle, they stopped, still holding hands. Grandmother quickly *whai*ed with great respect. With tottering steps, she moved forward and knelt on the ground before the King. Her head and hands touched the ground in honor to her King.

A hushed silence fell over the crowd. The King spoke. "You should have pride in your grandson who has not only helped bring good fortune to our nation but has also displayed great respect for his elders. He's a fine young man."

Grandmother slowly raised her body to a kneeling position, with her head still bowed. She seemed so frail and old . . . a small figure kneeling in the dust under the broiling sun. Those who could see her face watched large tears roll down her cheeks and fall into the dust.

The King turned and walked away. His beautiful Queen followed behind him. Boonmee's grandmother didn't move. Boonmee knelt beside her. "Grandmother, why are you crying?" he asked.

Between little sobs she replied, "Happiness, my son. Happiness. Today, I saw the King. I waited all my life to see our King."

Boonmee didn't answer. He had a lump in his throat for his grandmother. He knew she hadn't really seen the King. She had never raised her head the entire time so she couldn't have seen him. Boonmee wished that she wouldn't cry even if she was crying because she was happy. It hurt him to see her cry.

The crowd gradually disappeared. Boonmee guided his grandmother back to their family. Everyone was talking gaily. The village headman was explaining once again how his village had caught the white elephant. Boonmee listened for a while and then walked away.

He wanted to make one last visit to his little friend. When he went to the banana trees . . . White Elephant was gone. His little friend was gone forever. Boonmee sat down in the sand. He picked up a stick and began to draw sand pictures.

Boonmee's father watched his son drawing pictures of lotus blossoms and baby elephants in the sand. He was almost afraid to interrupt him. "Come, son. We must hurry to catch the bus. The last one leaves soon. We must hurry," explained his father, gently helping Boonmee to his feet.

Boonmee didn't speak, but walked silently beside his father. He was wondering where his little elephant would be sleeping tonight.

8

The King's Letter

THE DAYS were so long that every day seemed like a year to Boonmee. He missed his little elephant friend. Each morning and night he talked to his grandmother about the elephant.

"Grandmother, I miss my elephant so much," Boonmee said one morning.

"Boon, the little elephant misses you, too. He's just a baby and he's probably lonesome for you and for his mother. But he is now a royal elephant. He's an important elephant. He can't always do what he wants and be with whom he wants. Not now," answered his grandmother.

Whenever he rode on Buffalo's back, Boonmee thought of the day that he found the little white elephant trapped in the ravine. "I wonder if anybody plays with him or scratches behind his ears," Boon-mee asked himself.

He knew that he had to forget the little elephant, who now belonged to the whole Kingdom. But Boonmee still remembered how the elephant's pink nuzzle gave him wet kisses, and he was sad.

Then one morning, the Governor came to Boonmee's house with the village headman to bring Boonmee a message. The whole family gathered in the house to hear the Governor read the message:

> The Kingdom of Thailand is very proud of the new royal elephant, who is certain to bring good fortune. The elephant keeper reports that the elephant is very lonesome and isn't eating well. He thinks that a visit from Boonmee would make him feel better. On Friday of this week, a government car will pick Boonmee up and take him to Bangkok to visit the youngest royal elephant.
>
> His Majesty, KING BHUMIPOL.

All eyes were on Boonmee. No one spoke. Boonmee couldn't believe it! That had been the Loy Kathong wish he had wanted to make. He had waited a year to wish that he might go to the city at the end of the waterways.

"But, sir," replied Boonmee, "I gave up that wish at the Loy Kathong Festival. Instead I wished for the safety of the white elephant."

The Governor smiled at the boy sitting in front of him. "Well, Boonmee, maybe the Mother-of-the-Waters discovered your other wish, too. In any case, the King has invited you to spend several days in Bangkok. I'll be going with you."

"Imagine, our Boonmee being invited by the King," whis-

77

pered Grandmother to Boonmee's father. His father shook his head in a disbelieving fashion. There were tears in his mother's eyes.

The Governor continued, "The official car will arrive about seven o'clock on Friday morning at the main road where the bus stops. Together we will go to Bangkok. We should be there by late afternoon."

Not knowing what to do, Boonmee looked at his father. His father smiled and nodded his head. Boonmee turned to the Governor. "I'll be waiting for you, sir."

Boonmee's parents walked outside with the Governor, but Boonmee continued to sit on the floor with his grandmother. "Grandmother, I'll see my white elephant. I'm going to see my white elephant in two days!"

"Don't forget, Boonmee, he's not your elephant anymore. He belongs to the King and the Kingdom. Don't say *my* elephant anymore," said Grandmother sternly.

"Yes, Grandmother," replied Boonmee, lowering his head. He was embarrassed that he always called the little elephant *my* white elephant. "The King wouldn't like it if he heard me say that," thought Boonmee.

As soon as the Governor left, Boonmee's mother and grandmother began to make clothes for Boonmee's trip to Bangkok. Soon the other women of the village who had heard of Boonmee's good fortune came with cloth to help make clothes for his trip.

Boonmee wasn't worried about clothes. He was wondering if he would be afraid in Bangkok. He remembered Phra Kruu's stories. Bangkok was so big and very different from his village. He must go see Phra Kruu. Phra Kruu would know all the answers.

As soon as he entered the temple compound, he saw the monk. *79*

"I've been waiting for you, Boonmee," greeted Phra Kruu.

"Why?" asked Boonmee.

"I learned this morning that the King has invited you to Bangkok," replied the all-knowing monk.

"Phra Kruu, I'm scared. What do I do in Bangkok? Please tell me again about Bangkok and how to talk to the people there," pleaded Boonmee.

So Phra Kruu and Boonmee sat in the coolness under the trees. Phra Kruu again told the stories of the Kingdom's capital city. He explained that Boonmee should be polite and respectful to all people, just as he had been taught in the village. All afternoon Boonmee listened to the monk's wise instructions. It all sounded so simple when Phra Kruu explained it.

As Boonmee was about to leave, he turned to the Buddhist monk. "Phra Kruu, why did the Mother-of-the-Waters grant a wish I didn't make?"

"What do you mean?" questioned the wise monk.

"All year long I planned my wish for the Loy Kathong Festival. I was going to wish that I might go to the end of the waterways to see the marvelous things you have seen."

"What happened? Did you change your wish?" asked the monk.

"Yes. At the last minute I decided that I should wish for the baby elephant. He was scared and trapped, and I wanted him to be safe. So I changed my wish," said Boonmee, remembering that night.

"Fate has strange ways, Boonmee. There's nothing that we can do about it," instructed Phra Kruu.

The trees released sun patches that dappled and danced on Phra Kruu's saffron robe, making it golden. Maybe it was the sun playing tricks on Phra Kruu but the monk seemed taller to Boonmee,

80

and more regal, almost like a Buddhist statue, as he stood there beneath the trees.

Phra Kruu had noticed the boy wore the Buddha image which he had given him for his birthday. It dangled from his neck on a golden chain. Whenever Boonmee moved his body, it seemed to make a tinkle like the temple wind-chimes. Phra Kruu's smile changed to a look of serene contemplation as he watched Boonmee disappear through the temple gate.

9

A Wish Come True

BOONMEE'S new clothes, neatly tied up in his red and white sleeping sarong, rested in the grass as he waited by the roadside, holding his grandmother's hand. Many villagers had gathered to say goodbye to him.

At last the Governor arrived in a shiny official car. The driver, in an Army uniform, jumped briskly out of the car to open the door for the Governor. Boonmee's heart leaped into his throat, making a big lump. He was afraid.

The Governor greeted the village headman and Boonmee's family as the driver hustled Boonmee into the car. The car made a quick circle in the road and sped off. Boonmee waved frantically from the back window. Through the swirls of dust, he could see his family.

He continued to wave and look back until his family became specks among the banana trees.

He turned around and scooted down in his seat. It was a wide seat with a smooth leather covering. The Governor was reading papers, but occasionally he peeped over the rim of his glasses to look at the passing countryside.

Down the rough and dusty road they sped. Eventually they reached the big road. "This is Friendship Highway, Boonmee," instructed the Governor, peering over his glasses. "It was built by the United States many years ago. This highway takes us past the international airport and into Bangkok."

Friendship Highway was smooth and wide. Many trucks and buses whizzed by. Rice fields lined the highway as far as Boonmee could see. Small wooden boats loaded with fruits and vegetables drifted lazily down the *klongs* to the Bangkok markets.

Boonmee was tired and hot. He slid down in his seat, closed his eyes, and began to think of White Elephant.

The next thing he knew, the Governor was shaking him gently. "Boonmee, look over there. See the big jets. There's one taking off!"

A giant Thai International Jet Airliner raced along the ground and sprang into the air just before it came to a rice paddy. A thunderous noise made Boonmee put his hands over his ears. Long, black trails of smoke followed the big plane up into the sky.

Boonmee turned to the Governor, who was smiling. "It's noisy!" was all Boonmee could utter.

He now sat straight and rigid in his seat. Traffic was heavy. There were big trucks, crowded buses, cars, motorized *samlars*, motorcycles, and many people. The air was full of heavy noise, heat, and smoke. He suddenly wished that he had never left his village. He would get lost here.

There were red and green lights that made the cars and buses go and stop. The government car zigged and zagged through the streets, making Boonmee cling to the door. Their car halted abruptly in front of a huge iron gate. Four white-gloved soldiers saluted the car and waved the driver through the gate.

"The Palace Grounds," announced the Governor. "Take us to the royal elephant keeper," he told the driver.

Gone was the traffic and the noise. Cows were grazing beside the *klongs* that flowed among palm and coconut trees. "This is just like our village," said Boonmee, delighted that the driver was now going slowly.

"Yes, here in the Palace Grounds there are many acres of land for the King's royal cattle," explained the Governor.

"Look, those houses are just like houses in my village!" said Boonmee excitedly.

"Those are guest houses built in Thai style for visitors from foreign countries," explained the Governor. "Look over there. What does that look like?" he asked.

"Like an elephant. But it's made of a tree!" Boonmee responded.

"That's right. The gardeners cut the bushes and trees to look like animals. It's a Thai art," Boonmee's companion told him.

Their car stopped near a green tree elephant. "We'll get out here to meet the elephant keeper," the Governor explained to the driver.

Boonmee *whai*ed respectfully to the royal elephant keeper while the Governor explained that he would be back later to pick up the King's young guest.

Boonmee followed the elephant keeper to a large gate. "Your elephant friend seems to be lonely. He's too lonely to eat. Maybe you can make him happy again. I'm counting on you."

In a far corner of the field stood the small white elephant. Boonmee's heart sputtered with excitement, but the elephant looked so small. He wondered if this was the same elephant! His trunk hung down limply. His big, floppy ears drooped. He stood alone and sad.

"Go to him, Boonmee, and say hello. I'll bring water and food over. Maybe you can get him to eat something," the keeper said.

Boonmee put his bundle of clothes down by the gate. He was all alone in the field with his white elephant. "Will he recognize me?" wondered Boonmee as he walked toward the elephant.

He moved closer and closer, but the little elephant didn't respond. Boonmee stretched out his hand in greeting as he had always done, but the little elephant paid no attention. Boonmee spoke softly to him, as he had that day in the ravine. "Little elephant, it's me, Boonmee, your friend. I've missed you so much. Come, little one. Let's be friends again."

The little elephant's head swung slowly in Boonmee's direction. Boonmee continued to speak lovingly to him.

Then suddenly his little trunk went straight out. The pink nuzzle began to twitch and wiggle. "You recognize me! It's me! Boonmee! Come here! Come here!" Boonmee coaxed.

The little elephant's ears began to flap. One more large sniff, then he was certain. This was his friend!

Boonmee and White Elephant had found each other again. The little elephant's trunk wrapped around Boonmee in a happy hug, and Boonmee giggled as the elephant squeezed him tightly.

As the royal elephant keeper watched Boonmee feeding the smallest royal elephant, he began to formulate a plan. "I really need someone else to help with the royal elephants. I wonder. There's a school here on the Palace Grounds that Boonmee could attend. . . . Tomorrow, I'll speak to the King's secretary."

Boonmee sat crosslegged in front of White Elephant, feeding him hay by the handfuls. He thought about his family. He thought of his old grandmother.

A surprising thought came into his head. Why hadn't he thought of it before? "It was my grandmother. It was my grandmother

86

who made all this possible. It was the night of the Loy Kathong Festival when she made a wish for me with that raggedy lotus boat. Yes, it was Grandmother. She made her last wish in this life for me.

"That means that the Mother-of-the-Waters did hear my grandmother's wish. . . . But how? That funny-looking lotus boat must have floated all the way to the end of the waterways." Boonmee whispered his thoughts almost like a prayer.

He remembered the morning when Grandmother told him the story of the wish that did come true. It was a magical story. The world seemed so nice right now. That's the way Phra Kruu said it should be.

Tomorrow he would visit the city at the end of the waterways. He would hold everything in his head so he could tell his grandmother all about it. He would even draw pictures for her in the sand so she could understand. She would like that.

He tickled the elephant's pink nuzzle. "My little white elephant, they call you lucky, but it's really me . . . Boonmee . . . who is lucky!"

Boonmee, too, believed that a Loy Kathong wish could come true.